BUBBLE PIRATES!

Adapted by Mary Man-Kong

Based on the screenplay "X Marks the Spot" by Jonny Belt,
Robert Scull, Bob Mittenthal, and Michael Rubiner

Based on the TV series *Bubble Guppies,* created by
Robert Scull and Jonny Belt

Illustrated by Eren Blanquet Unten

A GOLDEN BOOK • NEW YORK

© 2013 Viacom International Inc. All rights reserved. Published in the United States by
Golden Books, an imprint of Random House Children's Books, a division of
Random House, Inc., 1745 Broadway, New York, NY 10019, and in Canada by Random
House of Canada Limited, Toronto. Golden Books, A Golden Book, A Little Golden Book,
the G colophon, and the distinctive gold spine are registered trademarks of
Random House, Inc. Nickelodeon, Bubble Guppies, and all related titles, logos, and
characters are trademarks of Viacom International Inc.
T#: 254124
randomhouse.com/kids
ISBN 978-0-449-81769-8
Printed in the United States of America
10 9 8 7 6 5 4

Molly, Gil, and Bubble Puppy were on their way to school when they saw a pirate captain. He was digging in the sand.

"Are you digging for treasure?" asked Gil.
"*Arrr!*" said the pirate. "But I can't find it anywhere."

"X marks the spot," squawked the pirate's parrot.

"You keep saying that," grumbled the pirate. "But I can't find the X."

"Do you have a treasure map?" asked Gil.
"Of course I do," said the pirate. "But I don't understand it."

"Look!" exclaimed Molly. "There's an X."
"Aye, that's where the treasure is buried," explained the pirate.

"I wish I were a pirate," said Gil.
"Me too," added Molly.
"Arf! Arf!" said Bubble Puppy.

The pirate captain had an idea. If the Bubble Guppies helped him find the buried treasure, he would make them proper pirates and share the treasure with them.

Molly and Gil couldn't wait!

Molly and Gil quickly swam to school. When they got there, they told all the Bubble Guppies about the pirate they had met.

Everyone was excited—especially when they saw the treasure map.

"What are those pictures?" asked Oona.

"Those pictures show landmarks," explained Mr. Grouper.
"Landmarks are things to look for along the way."
"Landmarks help you know where you are," added Nonny.

"And the X tells you where the treasure is buried!" added Gil.

Gil and Molly told their friends that if they could help find the treasure, the pirate would make them proper pirates for sure!

"Everyone who wants to be a pirate, say *'Arrr!'*" called Mr. Grouper.

"*Arrr!*" everyone shouted.

But Gil knew that to be proper pirates, they had to look like pirates.

So he swam over to Deema's Proper Pirate Store, where he found big pirate hats and awesome eye patches for everyone.

Now Gil and his pirate crew were
ready to search for treasure.

They looked at the treasure map. The
first landmark on the map was called
Spyglass Peak.

Gil spotted a mountain shaped like a
spyglass. "That's Spyglass Peak!" he yelled.
"Come on!"

After Spyglass Peak, the pirates worked their way to the second landmark on the map, Buccaneer Bridge.

"Careful, mateys! This is Buccaneer Bridge, and it's a long way down!" Gil said nervously, glancing below.

The pirates slowly made their way across the creaky bridge.

"Look!" cried Molly. "There's Parrot Rock! That's our last landmark!"

"That means we're almost at the X," said Gil. "C'mon, mateys!"

When they reached the X, the Bubble Guppies started digging for the treasure.

They dug deep, deep down into the ground.

"We found the treasure!" exclaimed Gil.

Just then, the pirate captain arrived. "Ahoy, mateys!" he called.

"We followed the map and found the treasure!" Gil told the pirate.

The captain was so happy. He made Gil, Molly, and all the Bubble Guppies part of his crew.

"Hooray!" they shouted. "We're proper pirates!"

Gil and his friends climbed aboard the pirate ship.
"I promised to share the treasure with you if you
found it," said the pirate captain. "You found where
X marks the spot, so let's open the treasure chest to
see what's inside, mateys!"

The chest was filled with something shiny and golden. It looked like a spoon— and also like a fork.

"It's called a spork," proclaimed the pirate. "X marks the spork!"

The Guppies laughed.

The Bubble Guppies sat down for lunch and passed out their golden sporks.

"What do pirates eat, anyway?" asked Molly.

"*Map*-aroni and cheese, of course!" exclaimed the pirate captain.

"*Arrr!*" agreed the Bubble Guppies.